MW00514330

Truly Leading

Lessons in Leadership

Finally, a book on leadership written by a man who practices what he preaches every single day. I found myself devouring every word and turning pages faster than I was supposed to in order to discover what pearl of wisdom Del would share next. Some people write books before their time, before they should and before they have anything meaningful to say. I applaud Del Suggs for living life to the fullest, mastering several career paths and THEN sharing what has helped him transform every life he touches —and he does.

In the world of speaking and entertaining it is nearly impossible to navigate the road to success unscathed. It is nearly impossible not to ruffle a few feathers, incite jealously or criticism or step on a toe or two. But in all my years of experience I have never heard a person utter an ill sentence or syllable about Del. On the contrary, people can't stop sharing testimonials as to how their life changed for the better from the moment they were fortunate enough to meet him.

One of my favorite quotes: "People should hear about you from everybody but you." I have never heard Del toot his own horn. I've never heard him take credit for something that was not directly his. I have never heard him say that his way was the only way, or even the best way, as he knows you can take many avenues to reach your final destination. Buy this book and read it once through without stopping. Then read it again, only this time with a highlighter and every time something touches you, or teaches you or inspires you, take note. Then, buy a copy for everyone you know and suggest that they do the same. You owe it to them.

David Coleman
"The Dating Doctor"
13-Time Speaker of the Year

Truly Leading

Lessons in Leadership

by

Del Suggs

Copyright 2011 by Delma Carl Suggs
All rights reserved.

No part of this book may be reproduced in any form, except
the inclusion of brief quotations in reviews, without the
express written permission of the author.

Suggs, Del
    Truly Leading: Lessons in Leadership / by Del Suggs

ISBN: 978-1-4507-6567-1
Library of Congress Control Number: 2011903467

Cover Design: Laura Pichard Murphy at Paisley Design.

www.DelSuggs.com

This book is available for quantity discount for bulk purchase.
For additional copies, contact:

Del Suggs
PO Box 2261
Tallahassee, FL 32316

Printed in the United States of America.
First Edition
April 2011

Contents

Acknowledgments

The Author would like to thank the hundreds of colleges and universities across the USA that have invited me to speak to your students. I also look forward to returning.

Thanks to my friend Dennis Haskins-- gifted actor, keynote speaker, and all-around good guy (who may have played "Mr. Belding" in *Saved by The Bell* at some point in his career) for writing the foreword.

Thanks to all the non-profit organizations and boards who gave me first-hand leadership experiences by inviting me to volunteer.

Finally, thanks to Denice. We're off on yet another adventure, aren't we?

Foreword

I've never met a finer person than Del Suggs.

He not only "talks the talk," he "walks the walk." Shake the man's hand, look him in the eye, listen to what he says, and know that he speaks the truth. His new book, "Truly Leading: Lessons in Leadership," defines the undefinable. He not only helps you understand leadership from every possible angle, he shows you how to practice it as well.

Del is one of the kindest, most supportive people I've ever met. When he asked me to write this foreword, I decided to look up his bio to learn even more about the man I already knew. I don't know where he has found the time to do all that he has done.

He is also one of the most humble. Del would never tell you all that he's accomplished, including the many awards he's received. But trust me, it's more than most people do in a lifetime and across the board in terms of experience.

He hasn't just studied what he writes and speaks about; he has lived it! This isn't just what one man believes; he lives it 24/7! If he says it, you can put it in the bank. It's true!

Knowing Del for as long as I have, one of the coolest things about him is that he has nothing in mind but your best interest. In this book he breaks down leadership in ways that not only help you to understand everything about it, he also shows you how to put it into practice.

Early on in this book, Del's favorite definition of leadership is "Leaders inspire others to know, to do, or to be." He also quotes a wonderful Japanese proverb, "'Fall down seven times, get up eight'. If you want to inspire others, do what you love and keep getting back up."

Del Suggs inspires me, and this book will inspire you to keep getting back up, too.

I highly recommend it!

Dennis Haskins
Hollywood, California

Preface

My life changed in the Fall of 2003. It didn't seem all that dramatic at the time. It was just another gig, a musical performance not too different from the 80+ shows I did every year at colleges across the USA. I was scheduled to play at the weekend Leadership Retreat for the district meeting of the Florida Junior/Community College Student Government Association. The District Coordinator booked me to play at their bonfire, and then as an afterthought, said "...and why don't you do a leadership break-out session, too."

I replied, "I don't know anything about leadership."

She said, "I've seen your resume. I think you do."

She knew that I had a lifetime of volunteer experience, and that I had served on the boards of various national and local non-profits. She saw something in me that I didn't know was there.

I drafted a program on the basics of leadership for my presentation. When the weekend was over, the students had rated it the best program of the entire retreat. I got the message, loud and clear.

In the few years since that retreat, I've traveled from Ft. Lauderdale to Seattle, from Laredo to Hartford, and most points in between, presenting Leadership Development programs for college students. I fly over 85,000 miles and spend over 135 nights in hotels each year. I must be doing something right: I was voted "Campus Speaker of the Year" by the school members of the Association for the Promotion of Campus Activities.

This book is a collection of quick lessons in leadership. While I hope you will find it a riveting read that you can't put down, it was really meant to be leisure reading. I know college students. You are busy with classes, studying, labs, writing papers and other academic requirements. Then you get deeply involved with campus programs, events, and organizations.   This volume is intended to be a guide, to provide a little training for those campus leadership positions.

It takes hard work to be an effective campus leader. Still, even with all the long hours and stress it can be fun, and it lays the groundwork for a successful future.   It's an opportunity to develop "transferable" skills, those abilities that will make you an exceptional employee, an extraordinary manager, and an even better person.

You'll find that the knowledge in this book will help you learn to work smarter and to lead quickly, efficiently, and effectively.   Whatever your leadership position on your campus, there is something here for you.

Let me know how this book helped you. Share your leadership experiences and lessons with me. Friend me on Facebook. Follow me on Twitter. Let me hear from you.

And, please invite me to your campus. I'd love to come and teach you to lead well.

Del Suggs
Tallahassee, Florida

"To lead people, walk beside them ... "
Lao-tsu

"Leadership cannot really be taught.
It can only be learned."
Harold Geneen

"It is no use walking anywhere to preach
unless our walking is our preaching."
St. Francis of Assisi

Truly Leading

Lessons in Leadership

Chapter One
Leading With Integrity

Leading with integrity is one of the great challenges of leadership. We often hear those phrases like "walk the talk" and "lead by example." Unfortunately, you can't just lead by cliché. You really have to "put your money where your mouth is," as the saying goes.

So, let's begin with defining our terms, starting with *Leadership.* Here are a few definitions that I like. Leadership is the process by which a person influences others or directs an organization. Or how about this: Leadership is the ability to facilitate action and guide change. But here's my favorite definition: Leaders inspire others to know, to do, or to be. Isn't that what we want to do as leaders? We want to inspire others to know, to do, or to be.

Integrity can be misunderstood. We think of integrity as a positive attribute. We say he or she "has integrity" as a compliment, meaning honesty and strong character. It's used as a virtue term. Actually, integrity comes from the same Latin root as "integer." You remember integers from math-- they are whole numbers. Integrity truly means whole, or complete. Consider leading with integrity as the proper combination of the two words: leading completely. It's a concept that we really need to ponder in order to understand. Perhaps a deeper consideration of leadership is in order.

Sources of Leadership

I believe that there are basically four sources of leadership. First of all, leadership comes from our **values and beliefs**. Our values are essentially our attitude about worth. What do you consider important, worthy, or of value? And our beliefs are the assumptions that we carry, perhaps understood as our convictions. Beliefs are also important because we compare every new experience against an existing conviction to evaluate it.

A second source of leadership is our **ethics and character**. Ethics is often confused with morality, or right and wrong. When I refer to ethics, I mean our conduct in a given situation. I think ethics is situational. People we consider to be ethical are people who behave consistently in the same or similar situations. Consider character to be a summation. It's the combination of your conduct, values, and beliefs.

Knowledge and skills are another source of leadership. Think of knowledge as the information you've learned or what you know. Skills are those abilities and capabilities that we gain throughout life. Certainly we look for our leaders to have knowledge and skills.

The fourth source of leadership is **authority**. We often think of authority as power, but that's not exactly right. Someone with power is just the boss. He or she may not have any real authority. I like to think of authority as power that we give to someone as a function of their position or job. Most of our elected officials have authority. We've given them power over us by voting them into office. When officials leave office, they tend to leave their authority behind for the newly elected official.

Add in Integrity

How does this discussion of the sources of leadership include integrity? It's pretty simple. While we can define the source of leadership, and even break it down into multiple areas as I've done, there is one more thing to consider. I call it the "gut check."

Designating leaders is not as simple as looking at someone's values and beliefs, ethics and character, knowledge and skills, and their authority. We all have this sixth sense, this personal intuition that we listen to when selecting leaders. When all is said and done, we trust our gut. We choose our leaders based on the obvious rational factors, but we supplement that with our gut feelings.

This is why integrity is so important. We seek leaders who are whole and complete, like integers. It's that integrity that grabs us. If there are two potential leaders with equal qualities in all other areas, we will choose to follow the leader with the most integrity. We make that decision in our gut.

Developing Integrity as a Leader

I can share with you a pretty simple formula for increasing your integrity as a leader. Understand that when I say simple, I don't mean easy.

There is a theory of leadership known as "servant leadership." I prefer the term "custodial leadership." It means striving to be the best caretaker, the best guardian, and the best keeper and protector you can be for those you lead. Servant leaders, or custodial leaders, govern with integrity. It comes from intrinsic core values, and a cognizant choice of service over self-interest.

Here's the three step formula for improving your integrity as a leader:

Step One: Seek the best for others.

Leaders with integrity ignore self-interest and personal gain, and seek to do the best for those they lead. Leaders with integrity are not the stereotypical boss, barking out orders for others to follow. Leaders with integrity are more like shepherds. They pursue the best for others, and watch after their flock.

Step Two: Practice good stewardship.

Leaders with integrity work to guard the resources of the group. That means spending funds wisely, using volunteers fairly, and properly utilizing and developing followers. Leaders with integrity are like farmers. They take care of the land, guard the crops, and maintain the resources.

Step Three: Never forget your constituents.

Leaders with integrity always keep their followers in mind. They are constantly looking for ways to lead, to take responsibility, and to do a better job as a leader. Leaders with integrity are like good parents. They are always thinking about their children.

Strive to be the best leader you can. That means leading with integrity.

Chapter Two
How to Inspire Others

There are people in our lives who lift us up. They may be personal friends, a teacher or professor, or someone famous. These people, whether or not they realize it, are important to you because they inspire you.

Inspiration is that feeling of enthusiasm and energy that we need to accomplish our goals. It's interesting to note that one common definition for inspiration is "the act of inhalation or breathing." Inspiration is just that important. Without breathing, we die. Without inspiration, our dreams die.

It's hard to explain, but you just feel better around some people, and that's due to their inspiration. While it may not be an intentional act, some people just exude inspiration. These people are not thinking "how can I inspire?" in their everyday life. They just do. They exhibit certain qualities and characteristics that make them a source of inspiration for others.

If you wish to inspire others, you've got to develop those qualities within yourself. It's not something we are born possessing, and even the most inspirational people you know had to learn how to inspire. If you want to learn, I've got some tips for you.

Be Positive

This is so obvious, yet so often overlooked. Is there anyone in your life who inspires you with his or her negativity? Of course not, unless you consider them a bad example. I always say: "Be Positive is not just a blood type."

We all need to believe. We need to believe that we can be successful, that we can achieve our goals, that life has meaning, and so much more. Belief requires that we be positive. We all have failures. Being positive requires that you work past those failures, put them behind you, and reassert your belief in the positive.

Make a conscious effort to reflect positively. Think positive thoughts, and block or correct negative images in your mind. Say positive things, and refrain from negative statements. Do it intentionally, and it will eventually become a habit, something you'll do without even realizing it.

Express Yourself

Display your passion, and others will be inspired. Enthusiasm is contagious. You've no doubt heard those impassioned speeches delivered by great coaches at half-time. You don't have to shout, scream, or cry to express your excitement. Express yourself in a way that is natural to you-- but be expressive.

Passion and enthusiasm cause curiosity. People will wonder why you feel so strongly about something, and they will begin to share your excitement.

Here's an example: I'm involved with a nonprofit that is doing wonderful work. We recently applied for a grant to fund an exciting community project, but we needed additional matching funds in order to receive the grant. I did a presentation for my local county government, and asked for $25,000. After I spoke, several county officers commented that they got excited about the project because of my enthusiasm. Needless to say, we got the funds.

Make a conscious effort to express your excitement and enthusiasm. You will find yourself inspiring those around you.

A Greater Purpose

Most, likely all, of the people who inspire you are dedicated to a higher cause. I'm not suggesting that you become a religious leader. I am suggesting that you reflect a dedication to a greater good.

Look at what drives you, what you believe in, what you see as your ultimate purpose. If your purpose is simply to make a lot of money and drive a cool car, you won't inspire others very much. If it's to make a lot of money so you can quit your job and build houses for Habitat for Humanity full-time, you will find that inspires others.

Simply put, self-centered and egocentric people don't inspire others. We are inspired by people who place others-- other people, other ideas, other goals-- above themselves.

Make a conscious effort to reflect on your higher purpose. That dedication to something bigger than yourself is inspirational.

Use BHAGs

I love this term, although it's become a bit dated. Corporations use this acronym often. BHAG stands for a **Big Hairy Audacious Goal**. It's a goal that's huge, a grand-slam home run, something that's unlikely but still possible.

Some people steer away from BHAGs. We're usually taught the idea of SMART goals-- another acronym that stands for Specific, Measurable, Attainable (or Achievable), Realistic, and Time-Based. Those basic standards help to assure that we can achieve a goal, and they are a good measure for most goals.

But BHAGs are special. It's those big, difficult goals that are inspiring. Consider this goal: to graduate from college. Is that difficult? Yes. Are others seeking that same goal? Yes, all around you. Is that inspiring to others? Not really, because it's such a common goal (unless you have extreme circumstances).

A BHAG is an inspiring goal. For example, to be the first person in your family to get a college degree. That will inspire others, and yourself.

Set a big goal for yourself, a goal that is a real challenge, a goal that you might not be able to achieve. You will find that a BHAG is an inspiration to you, and your efforts to achieve it will inspire others.

Use Short-term Goals Wisely

Short-term goals are the items on the daily "to do" list, those things we have to accomplish along the way to our bigger goals. Be aware of the immediate goals you have to complete, and always remember that they serve to reach the higher goals.

One excellent way to see the purpose of these little goals is to link them directly with your bigger goals, or even your BHAG. Imagine that your BHAG is to become a physician-- and that's a big goal. As you look at the steps involved, you will see that achieving your BHAG requires a lot of time in class, even early morning classes that you may detest. You might start by setting a goal of attending every class meeting of Organic Chemistry, even though it meets at eight o'clock in the morning.

Achieving that goal, simply showing up for class, will be inspired by the greater goal of becoming a physician. But attending every class will inspire your fellow students with your determination. It will inspire your professor with your drive. You will find that achieving those simple, short-term goals will inspire others, too.

Expect the best

It's important to demand your personal best in every situation. We're all inspired by people who have high expectations of themselves. Raise the stakes on your own work, and do the very best job you can every single time.

Part of the inspirational value of expecting excellence is with the people around you. If you expect the best of yourself, you'll find yourself expecting the best of those around you, too. And you will find that people respond in-kind. I believe people want to be held to a higher standard. If you expect the best from people, they will give you their best work.

Expecting the best from yourself and from others will inspire those around you. It's not a demanding, brow-beating expectation of excellence. It's the simple expectation that those around you are excellent, and will do their very best.

Be Consistent

Consistency is an under-appreciated inspirational quality. It's that ability to conduct yourself in a consistent, reliable manner that others will respect and appreciate. You may find that others will look to you when something important occurs, and they will observe your reaction before they display their own. The ability to maintain a sense of being calm and collected will reap great rewards, as others will seek to follow your example.

Consistency also includes the way you treat others. I believe that we should treat everyone as equals, from the school president to the custodial staff. Of course, I understand that showing respect for those in authority is also showing respect to the institution they represent. Still, be consistent in your treatment of others, people will be inspired by your consistent kindness and courtesy towards others.

Don't overlook consistency in your moral and ethical conduct. Nothing is more inspiring than someone who stands by his or her beliefs, and exhibits those beliefs in daily life.

You're a Coach

We are all inspired by our teachers and professors, those who seek to help us learn and improve ourselves; however, you should realize that you don't need a degree or a title to teach. We need to offer guidance to those around us when they need it.

Don't attempt to guide others without an invitation to do so, as it will be misunderstood. But always be open to questions, especially about your failures and successes, and be willing to help others to learn and grow. No doubt there were those who helped you in the past-- a mentor, friend, peer, or family member you could turn to when you needed guidance. Be willing to share your advice with others, and inquire about their progress.

Helping others to avoid mistakes, to grow and develop in their lives, is one of the greatest gifts you can offer. It will inspire others to help, too.

Keep an open mind

It has become one of the worst dilemmas of our time-- the refusal to change your mind. We see it all the time in our politicians generally used as a weapon against someone who does change. The facts don't matter once some people make up their mind.

Political enemies go after opponents because they "flip flop" on an issue. But isn't that what we really want? If you have an opinion, and you gain information that causes you to realize that opinion is wrong, then you should change your opinion. It's called an "Open Mind."

You should constantly be seeking new information. And if you get enough information to change your opinion, then by all means change it. You should certainly be able to explain your change of heart. Demonstrate an open mind, and inspire others to open their minds, too.

Recognize those who work hard and make a real effort

There is nothing so inspiring as true heartfelt gratitude. I believe that everyone feels a little under-appreciated. We all try so hard, and yet nobody truly realizes how hard we're trying. Or so it seems.

Recognize the people who are doing hard work. Acknowledge it to those around you. Let people know that you see they are working hard, and that you appreciate their efforts.

Here's a personal example: I was running one day for exercise. I was barely trudging along, really, as I'm not a runner-- just an out-of-shape guy trying to improve. Coming down the road I saw a bus, and it was the Florida State University Women's Track Team. I expected to feel totally humiliated, watching a busload of competitive athletes laughing at my futile efforts to get in shape. But when the bus came by, every single woman on the bus was smiling and giving me an enthusiastic "thumbs-up." They could see how hard I was working, and they wanted to acknowledge and encourage it. I was so inspired by their actions that I try to do the same thing in my own life.

Inspire others by recognizing their efforts, and acknowledging how hard they are trying. It's not about success, but about striving to succeed. That's the first step towards success.

Follow your Heart

Inspire others by doing what you love. I know it sounds easy to say. But learn to love what you do, or else learn to do what you love. Don't compromise.

If you do what you love you will inspire others with your perseverance, regardless of the level of success you achieve. When people doubt you, question your abilities, and watch you fail, you will persevere because you love what you are doing.

There is a wonderful Japanese proverb: "Fall down seven times, stand up eight." If you want to inspire others, do what you love and keep getting back up.

Chapter Three
Five Rules for Great Leadership

Writers love lists. I think there is something comforting about looking at a number of items that all relate to the same thing. Think about *The Seven Habits of Highly Effective People,* by Stephen Covey. Think of Gandhi's "Seven Deadly Sins." How about the "Ten Commandments," by Moses (okay, he had a co-writer).

I embrace list making in a lot of creative areas. For example, I'll often begin to write a new song by making a list. I'll write down every detail I can think of that deals with the idea or topic I'm developing. It gives me a foundation to both build on and to draw from during the creative process.

With a list in mind, this chapter is constructed on five ideas I hold as a basis for great leadership. I'm not excluding other ideas-- it's just that these five are important enough to use as the foundation.

Rule Number One: Seek and Take Responsibility

Think about the leaders you know and admire. Do they sit in the back of the room, with their heads down, hoping that they won't be noticed? Of course not. They are down front. They are quick to raise their hands when the opportunity arises. They are the first to volunteer.

Great leaders seek the opportunity to be involved. But they don't always want to be in charge. Sometimes they want to follow although they are generally among the first to offer to help. They don't hold back.

It's not always easy to be involved, and everyone is busy these days. Nobody has "free time." We're all booked solid. Yet, great leaders always find time to help. Whether it's with their job, or their club, or their friends, they always seem to find the time to step forward and help when they are needed.

It seems obvious that great leaders seek and take responsibility. In my experience, even the most successful organizations-- no matter how large-- are kept afloat by a smaller number of members. It's an eighty-twenty rule: eighty percent of the work is done by twenty percent of the membership.

Strive to be a part of that small group that truly contributes to the organization. Whether you are an officer or committee chair, or just an active volunteer without a position, make it your goal to become more involved. Look for opportunities to be responsible.

Rule Number Two: Dream Big

When it comes to goals, we've had the SMART mantra pounded into us. You know, your goals should be Specific, Measurable, Achievable, Realistic and Time-based. It's a handy rule of thumb when it comes to setting those organizational and personal goals each year.

That's a useful tool. But let me offer you another tool: Dream Big. Set an extraordinary goal, something that's not "smart." Set a goal that's a real long shot, something that's not easily attainable or realistic. Companies sometimes call them "BHAGs"-- big, hairy audacious goals.

Why would you want to set an impractical goal? For one simple reason: big goals are inspiring.

It might be difficult to make that 8 am. Organic Chemistry class if your only goal is to pass. You might be more inspired to get up early and study if your goal is to be a great heart surgeon. Sure, medical school could be years away from now, and practicing medicine even further away if you plan to specialize in surgery, and then in cardiac surgery.

Having that big goal may make the difference between actually getting up and going to class or sleeping in and just barely passing (or flunking). It helps to be inspired.

When I was in graduate school, my fellow grad students had an expression to deal with all the tedious busy work we were assigned: "Anything not worth doing is not worth doing well." But when we were inspired by a big goal, we would come in early and work late doing all the little things it took to achieve it.

Come up with that organizational goal that will inspire your members. Having that big dream can make the mundane chores seem more important. Think of the difference it makes to have a big goal. Could you get your members to participate in a fund raising car wash if the goal was to take all of the members to see a movie?

Now, imagine if the goal was to take all of the members to the national convention in New York. See the difference? Inspire your members with a big goal. You just might attain it.

Rule Number Three: Take Risks

Great leaders aren't necessarily great gamblers. You've seen the poker tournaments on television. It takes a certain type of person to risk it all in the face of uncertainty. That gambler isn't likely a great leader.

You've no doubt heard the expression "no guts, no glory." A calculated risk is almost required in order to achieve anything worthwhile. Note my use of the word "calculated" to describe the chances taken.

Great leaders look at all angles of a situation or issue. They consider the choices to be made. They look at the likelihood of success and failure. They carefully look at both sides of the equation. Then, fully informed and aware of the situation, they will take a chance.

One of my personal heroes is Abraham Lincoln. He was a great leader who took calculated risks. When Lincoln was inaugurated, he actually named leaders from the opposition party to his cabinet.

Why would he give his political enemies such power? He knew it was risky, that they might work against him or try to discredit him. But he understood that these leaders truly loved America and that they would serve their country regardless of how they felt about him. Just as importantly, he knew that they would always make sure he knew the other side of any issue. These weren't "Yes Men," because they would frequently disagree on the issues facing the country.

Make sure you do the research first, and learn all you can about any issue you face. Great leadership involves taking chances and doing some gambling, but until you've come to grips with the potential for success and the possibility of failure, you can't make a wise decision.

Sometimes that wise decision will involve risk. Don't be risk averse. All achievement involves risk. Be knowledgeable and aware, but don't be reckless. When you must, take risks.

Rule Number Four: Perception is Reality

Perception is really all we know. If we aren't aware of something, it might as well not exist. So for all intents and purposes, perception is reality.

What does that have to do with great leadership? Great leaders are perceived to be great leaders. In order to be effective, a leader must be followed, and people only follow those they believe are leading.

Under the British Parliamentary system, the Prime Minister rules until the end of the term or until a vote of no-confidence is called. That happens when the PM is no-longer perceived to be the leader.

Whether an election is called or not, the very same thing happens in every organization. The officers lead only as long as they are perceived to be the leader. This means you must maintain your perception as a leader in order to lead.

We know how important this is from the media around us, and from our own elected leaders, but it works on the smaller scale within organizations. The leader must make the right choices, set the right goals, appoint the right committee chairs, and set the right tone for the organization.

This means that as a leader, you've got to be confident and positive. No one wants to follow a leader who isn't sure where he or she is going. Now, which of us hasn't felt reserved, or unsure on occasion? But in order to be a great leader, you've got to reinforce your image as a leader. You can't always be the leader you want to be, and sometimes you might have to "fake it." Don't worry, I've found that great leaders are often great actors, also.

Model yourself after a leader or leaders that you admire. Emulate their qualities. Be wise and reflective but also decisive when the time is right. And, as the saying goes, be strong enough to be gentle when it's necessary. That means asking for advice and help when you need it. Keep reinforcing the perception that you are a leader, and it will become the reality.

Rule Number Five: Make It a Better World

Most great leaders choose to become leaders to make a difference. Great leaders are inspired by a challenge, a need, a problem, an issue that needs to be corrected. If you've read *The Leadership Challenge* by Kouzes and Posner, they refer to it as "Challenging the Process."

It can be a frustrating experience to deal with the status quo. The laws of physics that deal with inertia also apply to humans, such that situations tend to remain the same over time. It takes a strong, concerted effort to have an impact on any situation.

This frustration often leads to two common reactions. One is to simply give up. This is easy to understand, because it takes so much effort to produce any lasting change. Some potential leaders just walk away from the challenge.

The other reaction is to give up on the process. We see it all around us. There are those who are disenfranchised by choice, and who have gotten so frustrated that they no longer bother to work for change. Some of them don't even bother to vote.

Embrace the challenge that inspired you to become a leader. That can mean embracing a flawed system and working to reform it. That can mean working on a problem from the inside out.

Work to make a difference and have a positive impact. You can make it a better world.

Remember the famous words of anthropologist Margaret Mead, who said:

"Never doubt that a small group of thoughtful, concerned citizens can change the world. Indeed it is the only thing that ever has."

Chapter Four
Interpersonal Skills

What are interpersonal skills? These are the skills that enable you to get along with others without any personality conflict. These skills will help you build good working relationships with your fellow students, instructors, employers and business associates.

Working well with others involves understanding and appreciating individual differences. Therefore, interpersonal skills play an important role in determining how well you manage your interactions with others.

Interpersonal skills include the habits, attitudes, manners, appearance, and behaviors we use around other people which affect how we get along with them. We sometimes don't understand how important interpersonal skills really are. It's easy to laugh and make jokes about people who obviously lack interpersonal skills. But sometimes we need to examine our own impressions on others to better prepare for success in life as well as for a productive career.

The development of interpersonal skills begins early in life and is influenced by family, friends, and our observations of the world around us. Many of these characteristics are passed along to us by our parents or guardians. Some aspects of interpersonal skills may even be inherited.

To improve our interpersonal skills, we must first be aware of what we are like from the perspective of the people who interact with us. Habits of which we are unaware, actions which we think go unnoticed, and other things about us that might affect other people are impossible for us to change if we are not aware of them. One of the things that teachers try to do, starting in the early grades, is to help students correct bad habits and to develop good interpersonal skills.

As we mature into adults, it becomes our own responsibility to initiate any changes in interpersonal skills that might be needed. These skills are more important than ever and they greatly influence both opportunities and success. It's just that rather than trying to change interpersonal skills, as is the case when we are children, adults tend to make judgments about one another based on interpersonal skills without explicitly saying that is the case.

Try these helpful tips for improving your interpersonal skills:

Smile.   Few people want to be around someone who is always down. Do your best to be friendly and upbeat with those around you. Maintain a positive, cheerful attitude about school and about life. Smile often. The positive energy you radiate will draw others to you.

Be appreciative. Find one positive thing about everyone you deal with and let them hear it. Be generous with praise and kind words of encouragement. Say "thank you" when someone helps you. Make colleagues feel welcome when they call or stop to talk with you. If you let others know that they are appreciated, they'll want to give you their best.

Pay attention to others. Observe what's going on in other people's lives. Acknowledge their happy events, and express concern and sympathy for difficult situations such as an illness or death. Make eye contact and address people by their first names. Ask others for their opinions.

Practice active listening. To actively listen is to demonstrate that you intend to hear and understand another person's point of view. It means restating, in your own words, what the other person has said. In this way, you know that you understood their meaning and they know that your responses are more than lip service. Your friends will appreciate knowing that you really do listen to what they have to say.

Bring people together. Create an environment that encourages others to work and play together. Treat everyone equally, and don't play favorites. Avoid talking about others behind their backs. Follow up on other people's suggestions or ideas. If folks see you as someone solid and fair, they will grow to trust you.

Resolve conflicts. Take a step beyond simply bringing people together, and become someone who resolves conflicts when they arise. Learn how to be an effective mediator. If friends bicker over personal disagreements, arrange to sit down with both parties and help sort out their differences. By taking on such a leadership role, you will garner respect and admiration from those around you.

Communicate clearly. Pay close attention to both what you say and how you say it. A clear and effective communicator avoids misunderstandings with others. Verbal eloquence projects an image of intelligence and maturity, no matter what your age. And don't forget to "filter" yourself. If you tend to blurt out anything that comes to mind, people won't put much weight on your words or opinions.

Humor them. Don't be afraid to be funny or clever. Most people are drawn to a person that can make them laugh. Use your sense of humor as an effective tool to lower barriers and gain people's affection. Just be careful that your humor is tasteful. Off-color jokes of any kind will repel people from you.

See it from their side. Empathy means being able to put yourself in others' shoes and understand how they feel. Try to view situations and responses from another person's perspective. This can be accomplished through staying in touch with your own emotions; those who are cut off from their own feelings are often unable to empathize with others.

Don't complain. One of my favorite bars has coasters that say "No Whining." There is nothing worse than a chronic complainer. If you simply have to vent about something, save it for your journal. If you must verbalize your grievances, vent to your personal friends and family, and keep it short. Spare those around you, or else you'll get a bad reputation.

Interpersonal skills are how you are evaluated by everyone you meet, and everyone you know. Make sure that your skills create a good impression.

Chapter Five
Effective Time
Management

There never, ever, seems to be enough time to do everything that needs to be done. Time management is a skill that many of us need to develop. Here are some ideas to help you improve your own time management.

First of all, understand that you can't actually manage time. The clock ticks off seconds regardless of anything that you do. What we refer to as time-management is really managing the events and activities that go on in our lives.

Taking the time to improve your time management skills can lead to:

- the elimination of procrastination
- getting more done in less time
- less worrying about deadlines
- more productivity
- more relaxation time
- an overall increase in time.

Time management is a skill that takes time to development and perfect. It also is a skill that is different for everyone. Your best bet is to try a variety of different approaches until something clicks in your brain and sticks in your routine.

Here are a handful of tips to consider:

1. Make Lists: Write down as much as you can. If you don't carry a planner or notebook already, start now. I simply use a legal pad, so I'm not trapped into the boxes and forms that more formal "Day Planners" use.

A simple "To-Do" List is often a huge help to anyone, and I heartily recommend it. Your goal is to get everything down on paper so you can prioritize.

2. Make Use of Down Time: Use walking, driving, showering, or otherwise "dead" times to plan. Think about what your goals are for that day or the next. Which goals are most important? Prioritization is the key.

3. Reward Yourself: Whenever you accomplish something, especially the important things, make sure to take the time to reward yourself. A *Clockwork Orange* author Anthony Burgess' used the "Martini Method" to get things done. Burgess set a goal of 1,000 words per day. When he finished his word count, he'd relax with a martini and take the day off. Maybe a martini isn't the ideal reward for some of us, but the method stands useful.

4. *Concentrate on One Thing*: The human mind works more efficiently when it is focused. As we've seen before, multitasking is actually a hindrance to productivity. Focus on one thing and get it done. Take care not to bleed tasks into each other. At times, multitasking may seem like a more efficient route, but it is probably not. When you change tasks during multitasking, there is a lag in activity and focus as your mind comes back to the current task. You'll find you're more productive if you do one thing at a time.

5. *Avoid Procrastination*: When trying to be more productive and trying to save time, procrastination should be avoided like nothing else. It is the ultimate productivity-killer. Find ways to eliminate stalling and postponing of both decisions and actions.

6. *Set Personal Deadlines*: I love deadlines. A guaranteed way to alleviate some stress is to set your own earlier deadlines. Be realistic but demanding of yourself. Challenge yourself and, referring to tip 3, reward yourself for meeting a difficult challenge. Not only will this save you time and make you more productive in the long run, but you will also have a buffer time with little to no penalties compared to those received for missing a real deadline. Of course, this tip has potential for abuse, so be sure to make your own penalties for missing your personal deadlines.

7. *Delegate Responsibilities*: It is common for leaders to take on more than they can handle. The overestimation of your own abilities, though not necessarily a bad thing, can often result in stress and more work. Don't feel bad about delegating tasks. Most people want to help.

8. *Set up a Long Term Planner:* In our everyday life, we can often lose sight of our big goals. Setting up a long term planner will help you envision your long term goals and rationalize your current objectives. You may occasionally find yourself thinking "Why am I putting myself through this work right now?" If you take a look at your long term planner you'll be reminded that you are working to pay off your car or save up enough money for your college tuition. Revise this long term planner monthly to keep goals up-to-date.

9. *Work in a Team:* Although giving up responsibilities is a scary thought for some, it is an invaluable method to increase the productivity of everyone involved. Be sure the team goals are clear and that everyone knows who is responsible for given tasks. Make sure all lines of communication are open at all times. Give tasks to those who are best suited for them and things will get done faster.

10. *Be Careful to Avoid Burnout:* Burnout occurs when your body and mind can no longer keep up with the tasks you demand of them. Don't try to force yourself to do the impossible. Delegate time for important tasks, but always be sure to leave time for relaxation and reflection. Review your recent accomplishments and enjoy your success. Review and reflection is one of the best ways to gain confidence and higher confidence means more productivity.

You can't create more time, but you can use the time you have wisely. Manage your time-- and your tasks--

well. That will result in more time for you to do the things you want to do.

Chapter Six
Personal Goal
Achievement

There is one sure-fire way to be successful: start off with an action plan. We all want to be successful. Often, we just don't know how to be successful. That's why goal setting is so important.

Achievement at the personal level is keenly linked to goal setting. Until you've set a goal, you don't know where you want to go. In some ways, goals are maps that lead us to success.

But what are goals, really? And how do you set them?

Let me share with you some insights into goals and goal setting that I've learned and applied to my own career.

Goals Are Specific

First of all, goals are specific. The more specific you make your goals, the more likely you are to achieve them. That means specify every part of a goal. Don't just say, "my goal is to graduate." Be specific: "My goal is to graduate in (month and year) from State University with a B.A. in Accounting."

Here's another example: turn "I want a car" into "my goal is to buy a (year) BMW SUV in December of (year)." Go ahead and include the model and the color! The more specific, the better your goal is stated.

The clearer your goal is stated-- that is, the more concrete and specific-- the more likely you are to achieve it. Make sure your goals aren't just dreams. Make them real.

The Written Word

What's the difference between a dream and a goal?
Ink.

That's right. Goals must be written down. It may not sound logical, but think of it this way: your dreams are just thoughts, basically chemicals and electrical impulses dancing in your head. You can't see them or touch them.

When you write a goal down on paper, it becomes real. You can see it. You can hold it. It's a real, genuine, physical object.

It's that reality that makes dreams into achievable goals.

The concept of writing your goals draws, in one sense, on the work of Dr. Edward Banifield at Harvard University. He spent a lifetime studying people and behaviors, and reached many startling and controversial conclusions. Generally considered a conservative thinker, he is really beyond the realm of conservative and liberal ideologies.

One of Dr. Banifield's most important and profound studies dealt with the financial success of individuals. In an effort to learn the root cause of poverty, he sought to determine the factors that related to the acquisition of wealth. He studied the impact of family background, education, intelligence, influential contacts, or some other concrete factor that might influence financial success.

His conclusion was what he called "long term perspective." Successful people set future goals and they work to achieve those goals. It turns out that if you set a goal, and then pursue that goal, you are very likely to be successful. Who knew success was that simple?

Cursive Handwriting

When you write down you goals, do this: use cursive handwriting.

You're familiar with the left and right hemispheres of the brain. The left side controls analytical, practical thought. The right side controls artistic, creative thought.

When you write in cursive, you are actually using both sides simultaneously. So you are using both halves of your brain to achieve your goals.

Just apply this technique, and see how well it works!

Secrecy

When you create your goals, keep them a secret.

What do I mean by secret? Just that. *Don't Tell Anyone.*

Now, if you are changing majors, you'll have to tell the registrar and your adviser, of course. But don't reveal your goal to anyone who doesn't have to know.

Here's why: there is a proven psychological concept called "social reality." This concept, as researched and proven, concludes that stating an outcome to others leads to a premature sense of completeness. In other words, if you talk about it, your mind thinks you've already done it.

Back in 1933, Dr. Wera Mahler found that announcing the solution to a problem and having it acknowledged by others turned the idea into a social reality in the brain, even if it hadn't been accomplished.

Dr. Peter Gollwitzer is an expert in this field. In one study, four different tests of 63 people found that those who kept their intentions private were more likely to achieve them than those who went public and were acknowledged by others.

Telling others of your intentions gives you a "premature sense of completeness." So keep your goals to yourself!

Toss in a Ringer

It feels good to succeed. Success generates more success, so always have some immediate, attainable short term goals. These goals should be an important step toward achieving your long-term, bigger goals. Achieving a goal-- and quickly-- shows you can succeed.

How about this goal: Add fifty quality friends to your Facebook page this month. Note I said *quality*. Find some new Facebook friends who lift you up and teach you new things.

Achieving a goal, even if it's simple or small, encourages you to take the next step and pursue the bigger goals. Develop your goals as a hierarchy, so that you can complete the smaller, easier goals that will contribute to achieving your larger goals.

Lighten Up

You've got to be positive about yourself to achieve your goals. It's not always as easy as it sounds. As I say, "Be Positive" is not just a blood type. It's the real key to success.

If you have the "Eeyore" tendency (remember "Winnie the Pooh"), then the first step towards being positive is to stop being negative. Stop beating up on yourself. Self criticism serves no useful purpose. It only makes it less likely that you will achieve your goals.

If you are surrounded by Eeyores, then you might want to make one of your immediate goals to "accentuate the positive" and "eliminate the negative" as the old song says.

Here is a simple way to emphasize success. Each day, list five positive things that you have done today. They can, and should, be simple: "went to the gym," or "studied for two hours," or "cleaned up my room." Anything that is a positive success. Even the most negative personalities will be amazed at how many positive things they accomplish on a daily basis.

You ARE Successful!

Every small success makes the next big success possible.

But remember this: they are **your** goals. You created them. That means you can change them. During the year, you might decide that one or more of your goals isn't appropriate or worth the effort to achieve.

Perhaps, as you've taken classes and studied in a particular field, you've learned that the reality is different from your original impression. Maybe you found something else that excites you more than your original goal. Whatever the reason, understand that it's permissible to modify, change, or delete your goals.

After all, they are your goals. They aren't carved in stone. They are ink on paper.

Written in cursive handwriting.

Chapter Seven
The Art of Delegation

Why is delegation important? One of the most crucial and challenging tasks for leaders and supervisors is to share the work among those they manage and supervise. Leaders complain that they are tasked with workloads which exceed the time they have to complete them. Unchecked, this feeling leads to stress and ineffectiveness. In many cases, organizational leaders could greatly reduce their stress by practicing the critical management skill known as *delegation*.

Delegation is not what most people think it is. It's not simply assigning a task to someone else. It is, rather, the assignment of the authority and the responsibility to another person to carry out a specific task. The person who delegates the work remains accountable for the outcome of the delegated work, but the responsibility for completing the work shifts to the subordinate. Delegation empowers a subordinate to make decisions. For all practical matters, it is a shift of decision-making authority from one organizational level to a lower one.

The opposite of effective delegation is micromanagement, where a manager provides too much input, direction, and review of delegated work. If you've ever been told what to do, and then been told how to do it, then you know all about micromanagement.

If you're not sure when to delegate, then consider these questions:

1. Are you are spending too much time on day-to-day tasks with no time to think about the big picture?

2. Do you have someone working for you who could do higher value work?

3. Can you can see the potential of someone and you will lose that person unless his or her skills are utilized?

4. Do you need a new way of tackling a task that comes up regularly?

5. Do you want to see what a promising person is capable of doing?

If you answered "yes" to any of these questions, then you need to begin delegation.

Basics of Delegation

Delegation involves three important concepts and practices: **responsibility,** **authority,** **and**

accountability. When you delegate, you share responsibility and authority with others and you hold them accountable for their performance. The ultimate accountability, however, still lies with you. You should clearly understand that:

Responsibility refers to the assignment itself and the intended results. That means setting clear expectations. It also means that you should avoid dictating to the employee HOW the assignment should be completed.

Authority refers to the appropriate power given to the individual or group including the right to act and make decisions. It is very important to communicate boundaries and criteria such as budgetary considerations.

Accountability refers to the fact that the relevant individual must answer for his or her actions and decisions along with the rewards or penalties that accompany those actions or decisions.

Here is a step-by-step method for delegation.

Step 1. Determine the task. That means determine exactly what you want accomplished, your expectations, your requirements, and more. Be as exact as you can be with the outcome.

Step 2. Choose the correct person for the job. You know your subordinates. Make the choice wisely, based on his or her interest and ability.

Step 3. Meet with that person. Explain the task at hand, and explain why you have selected him or her to do the job.

Step 4. Make sure that the subordinate understands the assignment. Notify any one affected by the transfer of authority.

Step 5. Ask the subordinate how he or she will perform the assignment, perhaps asking what his or her initial approach will be.

Step 6. Listen actively to his or her response.

Step 7. Confirm their commitment to the task, and offer any assistance he or she might need.

Step 8. Let the person know that you are confident in his or her ability to complete the task you have assigned.

Step 9. Create checkpoints and a time line for completion of the task. This gives you the means to monitor his or her performance.

Step 10. Observe the checkpoints, and resist the urge to micromanage.

Step 11. Recognize and reward the person when they complete the assignment.

When you begin to delegate, you may find that it's not as easy as it sounds. Often it seems that delegation is actually more difficult than simply doing the task yourself. If you find that to be true, then consider these pitfalls of delegation. Here are some common mistakes:

Reverse Delegation is when the person you've assigned the task is constantly coming to you for guidance and input. You end up doing the task yourself. This is sometimes known as "upward delegation."

Dumping is when the person you have assigned the task feels like you have simply lightened your load by dumping a dirty job on them.

Grabbing the Glory is when the person you've assigned the task completes it, and *you* take the credit.

Delegation is a wonderful opportunity for subordinates to learn new skills and develop confidence.

Never forget that delegation is essential. No leader, regardless of his or her gifts, can do it all. You need help, and you've got gifted people around you. Learn to delegate properly.

Chapter Eight
Being A Better Leader

Happy New Year! Okay, so it's not actually January 1. But remember that every day is a fresh start, and a chance for you to begin anew. With that in mind, let your "New Year's Resolution" be to do a better job leading your organization. Here are some great ideas for improving your leadership skills, and improving the effectiveness of your organization.

Communication

Resolve to do a better job communicating. Today we have access to incredible communication technology, yet we seem to be even more out of touch. Use your email, your cellphone, and your IM to keep your members better informed about upcoming events and meetings.

Set up a listserv or simply an email list for all of your members.   Keep everyone informed of ongoing discussions, upcoming deadlines, and the constant concerns of your student leaders. It is so much easier to make decisions when your executive committee and your general members are kept in the loop. Communicate!

Office Hours

Just a few years ago, organizational officers had to be in an actual office to make phone calls and conduct business. Today, we can do business from anywhere-- which is why it is even more important to maintain office hours.

You should designate regular hours each week when you will be in your office. Use that time to focus on board business, return phone calls, reply to emails, read your mail, and all that other boring stuff that is so easy to put off. By setting and keeping office hours, you'll be more productive, more informed, and a better leader for your organization. Your office hours are not the time for doing class assignments, surfing the Internet, or text messaging your friends.   Use the office hours as an excuse to concentrate on your job of leading the organization. Take care of business during office hours, and you'll be amazed at how efficient you can be.

Meetings

There are many ways to improve your meetings, and make them more effective for you and your organization. Some very simple actions can lead to big results.

Set up a regular meeting schedule, such as every Tuesday at 7 pm. If you always meet on the same day and time, it becomes part of your members' schedule. Attending will basically become a habit.

Set a beginning and ending time for each meeting, and stick to it! Your members will give you a certain length of time, but everyone hates those open-ended meetings that go on forever. Your members are far more likely to attend a meeting if they know it will only last for one hour.

Email out the meeting agenda in advance, so your members will be informed and ready to act.

Have an anticipated action for each agenda item. For example, don't just list "Fall Festival" as an agenda item. Include the action you plan to take: " Fall Festival: Select the Band" is a far better agenda item.

Keep accurate minutes of each meeting, and send them out with the agenda in advance of each meeting. That will keep everyone informed about board business, and upcoming decisions.

Appreciation

Everyone likes to feel appreciated, and your members are no different. Effective leaders express their gratitude strongly and openly. Think about the ways you express your thanks to your members. Does it really reflect your thankfulness for their work? Come up with new ways to say "thank you."

Write thank you notes. Everyone appreciates a handwritten note. How about a thank you gift? It doesn't have to be expensive to show appreciation. Buy some movie tickets (sometimes you can even get them at a discount from AAA or your credit union!) or a meal card from a local restaurant. How about a nice fountain pen, for those fancy signatures? Go browse through the local Dollar Store-- you'll be surprised at all the cool stuff you can get for a buck.

Try something clever and creative. Thank your members for completing a major assignment by giving them a gift-wrapped bottle of aspirin and antacid tablets, and thank them for eliminating your headache and indigestion! They will know you appreciate their work, and who doesn't need some aspirin at some time?

Eliminate Committees

Can you hear the cheering from your organization when you announce that you've abolished committees this year? Nobody likes to serve on committees. They meet too often, for too long. They never get anything done, and once you get on one you can't ever seem to get off the committee. Well, bid committees goodbye!

This year, institute a "Task Force" system to meet your goals. How is it different from a committee? To begin with, a task force has a specific goal, such as produce Spring Fling, as opposed to the music committee which might have to produce numerous events. Second, it has a clear completion date. Your Spring Fling task force is over the day after Spring Fling!

You'll find it much easier to recruit members for a task force than for a committee. The assignment is clear, with a beginning and an ending, for a specific length of time. When the task is finished, then you can recruit good task force members to another new task. Give it a try!

Training

Make this the year that you begin some formal training for your organization. Plan a retreat at the beginning of the year to do team building with your members and teach them the skills needed to serve the organization.

If it's too late to plan a retreat at the beginning of the year, then hold a retreat at mid-year. There is no better time for training, because you will have already uncovered their weaknesses as a group. You may find board members who don't cooperate; here's the need for team building. You may find poor attendance at your events; here's your need to teach promotion and publicity techniques. By the middle of the year, you will plainly see what your organization needs in order to be more successful.

You may need to schedule your retreat at the end of the year. That is also an excellent time for training. Just make sure that you've already selected your new officers for the coming year. Then you can really take the lead in training them to do the very best possible job. Remember, there is no wrong time to do training.

Lead By Example

Let your final "New Year's Resolution" be to lead by example. We all seek two things from our leaders: Vision and Integrity. Demonstrate your vision clearly to your organization. Let them know your goals for the organization, and how you intend to achieve those goals. Demonstrate your integrity by the way you live your life everyday. That's what great leaders do.

Chapter Nine
More Effective Meetings

"I hate meetings!" Does that sound like your members? Unfortunately, meetings are a necessity. It's how we get things done. It's how we make things happen. It's how we consolidate our individual efforts into a more powerful force. If your campus activity board members hate to meet, then it's time to do something altogether different.

Many people get put in charge of an organization with very little training other than their own personal experience. That means it's hard to be a good chair yourself, even if you've experienced meetings with an effective chair. Meeting management skills must be developed and practiced. I thought I would share with you a number of techniques for more effective meetings.

Before the Meeting

Begin by "defining" the meeting. There are basically five purposes for any meeting:

1. To Exchange Information
2. To Make Decisions
3. To Solve Problems
4. To Explain Issues
5. To Share Concerns

Note that these are all "action" statements. Meetings are for action.

It is important for your members to know why they are meeting. If they don't know the purpose of the meeting, then they may skip it. Or, they may attend because they are required but not really participate. Make sure your meeting has a purpose and explain that purpose to your members.

Schedule the best time and place for the meeting. If you're in charge, it can be tempting to set the meeting time when it's most convenient for you. Remember that one major function of any meeting is to bring your members together. Make sure that the meeting is held at a time and place that is best for the majority. If there is not a single convenient time for every one, then rotate meetings so that the most members can attend the most meetings.

Set the beginning *and* ending time for your meeting. Your members are busy people. Their time is important. You will have more success with both attendance and participation if your members know how long the meeting will be. And here's a hint-: if you keep your meetings to one hour or less, you'll find them both more efficient and better attended.

Create and distribute your agenda in advance. Everyone attending should have a copy of the agenda well before the meeting. If you are handing out agendas to members when they arrive, you've missed any opportunity for any real preparation.

Have a "consent agenda." Reports from standing committees (or tasks force), minutes from previous meetings, the treasurer's report, and any other reports should be included in the consent agenda. Then, for the sake of brevity, you can simply move and second the consent agenda. There is rarely a reason to read the previous minutes or the financial report aloud when the members can review the material in advance. Of course, members can ask that an item be removed from the consent agenda for discussion, if necessary. Then you can move on to the important items on the agenda.

List an anticipated action for each agenda item. That explains why the item is on the agenda along with what action you expect from your board members. For example, don't just list an agenda item as "Spring Formal." State the action you expect: "Spring Formal: form task force of 5 members." Or, "Spring Fling Band: make final selection." You can have discussion or information items: "New Coffeehouse Program for Fall Semester: information and discussion." Having an anticipated action explains why these items are on the agenda.

During the Meeting

Take useful and pertinent minutes. Don't get sidetracked trying to document every single word spoken at your meetings. Make sure your secretary, recording secretary, staff member, or whoever is in charge of minutes captures the main ideas and tangents that occur. You must record any actions (such as motions, seconds, and votes) to demonstrate that proper procedures were followed. It's also important to include any items which will be discussed or resolved at a future meeting, and any assignments that are made.

Follow your agenda strictly. Don't allow new business to supersede the original reasons for the meeting. Don't let members interrupt the meeting with questions or information that is unrelated to the item at hand. Your members all received the agenda in advance. They should be familiar with the business to be accomplished. Therefore, you can move forward and call for the anticipated action with each item.

Adjourn on time, or agree to stay later. For example, twenty minutes before the scheduled end of the meeting, the Chair might say: "If we continue to discuss the bands we are considering for the Spring Fling, we will need to stay an additional fifteen minutes to select the members to attend the National Convention. Can everyone stay that long, or should we end this discussion and move immediately to that decision?"

Make sure that each member says at least one thing at every board meeting. While this is primarily the Chair's responsibility, everyone can help make this happen. For example: "Brittany, you haven't said a word on this. Who do you think should be the first performer in the new coffeehouse?".

Encourage "dumb" questions, respectful dissent, and authentic disagreements. We gain more from defending our positions than we do from simple agreement. Find a chance to be encouraging at every meeting: "Chip, that's not a dumb question. I didn't know the answer, either." Remember, too, that compromise is important, and that you will generally get a better program by combining ideas from different sources than just accepting the first concept on the table.

Set the time and place for the next meeting. If your organization doesn't meet regularly, then you'll need to set each subsequent meeting at the current one. While selecting the day, time and place for your next meeting, don't forget the members who are absent at this meeting. If some members are unable to meet on certain days and times, then schedule the next meeting at a time they can attend.

After The Meeting

Prepare the minutes promptly. It is important to capture both the facts and the spirit of the meeting as quickly as possible. That way, if the secretary has a question it will still be fresh in the minds of others who attended. If the minutes aren't written immediately you run the chance of missing not only the essence of the business but the actions that were taken as well.

Review and evaluate the meeting. How did it go? Did certain members dominate the discussion? If so, you may need to find a way to limit their input. Were there distractions from the agenda? Then find a way to keep your members focused and on task. Did the meeting run too long? Pacing is vital to keeping a meeting flowing, but remember to keep your agenda realistic. Trying to force too much content into a meeting can be a recipe for disaster.

Meeting Etiquette

There is more to an effective meeting than just the previous items. Those attending the meeting must demonstrate civility and consideration. Showing respect and courtesy is vital, especially since civility is a current national issue. As our actions rub against each other, manners serve as a social lubricant to smooth the friction of our lives.

Let me offer these suggestions to those who attend meetings. They are simple and obvious, thus they are frequently overlooked.

Be prompt. That means arrive early or on time, but don't be late. Latecomers delay the meeting, create confusion and interfere with the flow of business. Make it a point to be on time.

Avoid interruptions. Turn off your cellphone, don't log on and check your email, and put away the gameboy. You need to pay attention to the business before you.

Be cognizant of time. You should certainly say what you want, and participate in the meeting, but not to the extent that others can't get the floor. Don't dominate the discussion.

Refrain from distractions. Avoid whispering those humorous or obnoxious comments to your neighbor. Don't shuffle your papers, or use the meeting to sort your files and clean out your notebook. Don't pass notes and giggle.

Stay for the entire meeting. Don't slip out early. Important information is often announced during the last few minutes of a meeting. In fact, holding some items until last can be a good strategy by the Chair to keep members focused and present.

Show courtesy and respect for your fellow members, for the Chair, and for the organization you represent. And, while not everyone can learn to love a meeting, you can certainly make them more efficient and more effective. What's not to love about that?

Chapter Ten
Alternatives to Robert's Rules

Mention *Robert's Rules of Order* to any assembled group, and you will get a collective groan. *Robert's Rules of Order* is a part of our lives as leaders-- it's even written into the bylaws of most organizations. I'm often asked if there is an alternative to "Roberts Rules."

Yes, there is.

Many organizations across the country are adopting a meeting process called "Consensus." It's effective and efficient for most groups, and it doesn't require the learning curve of "Robert's Rules" for new members.

Robert's Rules of Order was first published in 1870, and incorporated the so-called parliamentary procedure as used by Congress. It was presented as the best way to run a meeting. Perhaps it is the best way to run large meetings, conventions, Congress, and other rowdy assemblies. But for smaller groups, it's rather confusing with its formal motions, debates, precedence of some motions over others, and more.

Consensus is a simplified method of discussing an issue and reaching an agreement. It is important to understand that consensus doesn't mean that everyone be in agreement. It does mean that everyone has to be willing to accept the agreement that is reached.

It works like this: an idea is brought to the floor. It doesn't have to be a motion, or even a formal proposal-- just an idea. The idea is discussed, and it will probably be improved from the input of others. When a general agreement appears, you test for consensus by stating the current version of the idea. If everyone agrees, you've reached consensus. If there is dissension, then you can continue the discussion until a more acceptable version is reached. When you've reached consensus, or when there is a willingness to accept the current proposal, then-- in those familiar parliamentary terms-- the "motion is approved."

In reality, this may likely be the way your organization already operates. Groups often reach consensus in discussion first, then revert back to parliamentary rules by asking the members for a formal motion, a second, then voting.

If you like the sound of this, then you need to go to your favorite search engine and do some research. The use of consensus is becoming increasing popular for less-formal meetings such as clubs, neighborhood groups, and other smaller gatherings.

Check this out, and see if this alternative to *Robert's Rules of Order* makes sense for your organization.

Chapter Eleven
Embracing Technology

In the past forty years, student leaders have embraced each new technological advance. Consider these particular changes: from manual typewriters to electric to the IBM Selectric. If you've never heard of it, the Selectric was a marvel. You could actually change fonts, and it would allow you to correct mistakes without erasing! How about the touch-tone phone? Compared to rotary phones-- waiting for the dial to rotate back around so you could enter the next number-- they were cutting edge. Then came the Facsimile Machine, the fax, when it had to be there even faster than Federal Express' overnight delivery service.

Tomorrow's student leaders will be even more dependent on technology than today's office. However, it will likely have even fewer machines. In the near future, most "office equipment" will consist of two advanced machines: a computer (with broadband Internet and printer/scanner), and a cellphone. And it's likely that the smartphone may replace the computer. Those peripheral devices like printers and scanners may become unnecessary as we become a more "paperless" society.

Technological Compatibility

While there is some resistance to embracing the new advances, most students are ahead of the curve. It's refreshing to see the sea change in attitude. Student leaders are at the cutting-edge of the newest technology.

If college students and student leaders have access to the same technologies, then there is an extraordinary opportunity. One beautiful thing about this common technology is the way it can help create better campus organizations. Let's consider some of the most popular new opportunities that are useful in the world of campus clubs and organizations.

Facebook

Facebook is known as a social networking site. Basically, a student signs up, gets a free web page called a "profile," and can begin to start communicating with "friends" (other members). The attractive thing about these sites has to do with their interactive nature. "Friends" link to each other. They can link to other sites (YouTube, etc.) to share information. Music, photo, and video files can be linked and shared. Friends can essentially design their "space" to match their personalities and interests. This is how a lot of people make friends and communicate with their peers.

We're all familiar with the potential (and real) problems with these social networking sites. They have gotten a lot of bad press, and some of it may be deserved. But they are not going away. Students log on and stay on for hours each and every day. Users can set their own profile to private if they want, and keep any strangers from exploring their personal site without prior approval.

What can this mean to student leaders and their organizations? First of all, if you're not on Facebook, then log on and join. It's the only way to become familiar with the sites and their potential. You can't truly appreciate all they can do until you're involved. Don't worry, this is a legitimate consumer website. You won't be automatically branded as a predator just because you have a Facebook profile. I do-- and so do Stephen Colbert, Willie Nelson, Barack Obama, and most of the students on your campus.

You can set up a "Page" for your organization. It's really simple. Go to www.facebook.com and create a page. Then, invite the students in your organization to "like" the page and link to your site. Investigate all the different options for this social networking site. Once students are linked as friends, you can send out "Invitations" to your events. You can also link to the pages of programs and events you have scheduled so that your network of friends can learn about them.

While membership in this site is free, there is a service being offered by Facebook. For a small fee, you can send an electronic flier to every member of a specific group. For example, you could send an electronic flier announcing an upcoming event to every member who attends your college or university. That is some amazing target marketing!

Listserv and Electronic Mailing Lists

Before the advent of the world wide web, those with email capabilities often subscribed to electronic mailing lists. These mailing lists generally used the most popular software called "Listserv" first developed in 1984. The original use of listserv was as a mail reflector. Any member could send an email to the listserv address, and it would be resent ("reflected") to every other member. This enabled online discussion, with everyone having access to all information. Because members have to subscribe ("opt-in"), it's not SPAM.

You could have an electronic mailing list for your organization. Your members could sign up and receive emails about upcoming meetings and events. It's free. You can set up your own mailing list at Yahoo (www.Yahoo.com) and Google (www.Google.com).

Of course, if you set up your Facebook Page and your members all become friends then you can simply use it instead. The nice thing about an emailing list is that your messages don't get lost in the crowd of "status updates" as they can in FaceBook. Of course, it also assumes that your peers check their email regularly.

Text Messaging

Nearly all students "text" (that is, send text messages). You can see them thumb typing on their cellphones in class, in the student center, and even while walking across campus. If they are using text messaging so heavily in their personal communication, then your club should be using it to communicate with them.

Perhaps the simplest method is a service called "Mozes" (**www.MOZES.com**). You can set up an account, and Mozes will send your text message to every one who has subscribed to your texts.

It's simple. Open your free account, and get your "keyword" (like "MySchoolSGA" or "SAB") which identifies your account. At that point you're ready to text. Ask your peers to text your keyword to this number: 66937 (that's dialing MOZES on your phone keypad). They will receive your welcome text message and will be subscribed to your list.

When you want to send a text message to your "mob" (that's the term for your MOZES group), you log on to your account at the MOZES website and send it. All who have subscribed will get your text message on his or her cellphone. It's a bargain at $5 a month for your account.

There are a few other ways to communicate through texting. **www.Broadtexter.com** is a similar site to MOZES, except it's free. The downside is your members actually have to go to the Broadtexter.com site to register for your text messages. Remember, with MOZES they can sign up from a basic cellphone.

There is one more way to get a free broadcast texting system for your group. Don't laugh-- it's called "Twitter." You know about Twitter because it's so popular with the media, and not so popular with students, but it's a very effective means of broadcast texting.

Here's how: go to **Twitter.com** to create an account for your organization (we'll call it "Campus SGA"). Now, have your members text "Follow Campus SGA" to 40404. They will be signing up to receive your tweets. They don't have to create their own Twitter accounts. They will just get your tweets! Voila, instant broadcast texting!

Club Collaboration

The last new innovation I'll cover is online project management. That may sound confusing, but it's remarkably simple. Because your members' lives revolve around the Internet, they will grasp this quickly, and utilize it to the fullest extent once they understand what it does and how it works.

One of the most popular project management sites is **www.BaseCampHQ.com**. Anyone can sign up for the most basic service for free. If it proves useful you can expand into an account with more capabilities for a small monthly fee. And, it's a password-protected site, so access is only available to the people you allow to have log-in privileges.

It's very straightforward to work with BaseCamp. You set up your organization online. You can even upload your organization's logo, and it will personalize every page you use. Within the site, you'll have to-do lists, assignments, latest activity on the site, even a message board. Your club members can log on, get their assignments, then check them off on the list. They can communicate with you and each other on the message board, posting comments and concerns. It has a calendar for milestones, so you can set and meet your deadlines.

Here's a couple of things I love about BaseCamp. First, you can assign responsibilities to the to-do list. For example, if John is assigned to "Bring sponges to the Car Wash," he'll get an automatic email notice. Second, your scheduled meetings and other events will automatically trigger a reminder email to your members.

Your members, who even now are online most of each day, can stay as connected with each other as if they were sharing an office. It is a great use of technology that keeps everyone informed. BaseCamp may be the best way to deal with those communication problems that nearly always occur in group projects.

Getting In-- And Staying In-- The Loop

So, if any of this is new to you, here is your assignment: log on and explore. Sign up for a Facebook profile, and see how useful you find it for working and communicating with your members. See if you can't find ways to use it to inform them about your organization and events, and invite them to participate.

Set up your free broadcast texting account, get some students to sign up, and create your first "Flash Mob" (look it up!). Take your next big collaborative event (maybe "Spring Fling" or "Welcome Week") and put it online at BaseCamp. See how productive your student leaders can be when they are able to work whenever and wherever they choose-- in their dorm room, the library, or Starbucks.

You better learn this technology, because it will be with us for a while. You don't want to be one of those people whose VCR is always flashing "12:00" because they can't set the clock. If you embrace technology, then the VCR won't be a problem. You'll have TiVO.

Chapter Twelve
Successful Retreats

You have veteran members who know everything (just ask them!); you have new members who are green as a grasshopper; and, you have a few members who have been around just long enough to figure out they need a little guidance. They all need to learn to work together as a team, while at the same time they need to learn to perform their duties and responsibilities as leaders of your organization. Unfortunately, there is no time at the weekly meetings for any kind of training or bonding. What do you do? Sounds like it's time for a Retreat!

Retreats can be the perfect way to get your team in the game. You can teach new skills, create a sense of camaraderie, and take care of some serious planning. A retreat can be the solution to a number of problems, and it doesn't have to be done at the beginning of the year. A retreat held with the club members over the Summer or just before Fall classes begin can be a terrific time to schedule the first semester events. But a retreat held in January will allow you to address the deficiencies you've noted during the Fall, and serve to reinvigorate your board. Still, a retreat at the end of the year lets you recap your successes and failures over the last year while they are still fresh in your mind, and begin planning for next year's victories.

Start with some advance planning and analysis. Do you have a group with obvious weaknesses-- such as poor promotion, homogeneous programs, or just lack of motivation? Do you have some students who just don't get along, a "personality conflict" that flares up whenever they try to work together? Do you have some members who don't follow through and complete their duties, leaving you or other members to carry the load? All of these issues can be effectively addressed at a retreat. Make a list of your concerns, and present programs that will impart the skills your members need.

Next, look at your budget, and options. The ideal retreat is held away from campus or the office to eliminate everyday distractions. So consider going off campus, if possible. Perhaps your school has a place such as a camp or a guest house, or maybe even a meeting facility you could use. Maybe you could borrow or rent a place from a supportive alumni. Look hard, and don't rent a space unless you absolutely have to, because you can spend that money on other projects.

If you can't get off campus, try to get as isolated as you can. It's difficult to have a retreat in the same student center room the organization meets in every week because it may resemble a typical meeting. You need to find some place different. The school's Board of Trustees meeting room might be reserved through the President's Office, and it will certainly be a change from your office.

Consider your time frame and schedule. Don't be locked into false conceptions. Some wonderful retreats have begun on Friday afternoon and ended on Sunday night. Still others all occurred in one day. It's a matter of knowing what you need to accomplish, and finding a way to do the job.

If you have a brand new group, then you may need several days to teach them the skills they need. If you have a membership with mixed experience, then some skills can be learned from other members through an informal apprentice program. It's all up to you.

Retreats generally begin with some team building. You've got to allow opportunities for the group to get to know each other and to bond. That means icebreakers, games, athletic events, and more to facilitate a team interaction. Low ropes courses are popular, as are other semi-skilled athletic outings such as canoeing and hiking. But don't plan anything too strenuous or dangerous. You don't want your members too exhausted to participate in the training programs, and you certainly don't want any injuries!

A weekend retreat might have team building in the mornings, and training in the afternoon and evenings. Of course, you'll want to end each day with some fun. Whether it's 'smores around the bonfire, or a karioke dance party, let your members have some laughs. It's all for the sake of building camaraderie.

You've also got to do some honest-to-goodness teaching. One basic reason for a retreat is to educate your members about leading. There is much to learn, and there will be many different starting points. So let's begin by taking a quick survey of their strengths and weaknesses. Have they been having problems in specific areas? Are you worried about their lack of professional conduct, like making decisions promptly, returning emails and calls, and more? If you see some obvious shortcomings, then address these at the retreat.

Don't miss the opportunity to bring in an outside facilitator to help with your retreat. I frequently present sessions for retreats and workshops. One thing you may already know: students are more likely to believe something that someone else tells them-- even if it's the same thing they hear from you. It's funny, but true.

There are lots of ways you can use outside experts. With some trainers, you just get out of the way and they do everything. Other professionals may just present in their area of expertise. I find that the most effective retreats are jointly facilitated by a "visiting scholar" and the adviser. The adviser can utilize his or her skills and strengths, and bring in an outside expert to emphasize other important topics. Everyone needs to be involved. Team building isn't just for your members, It's for the leaders, too. You are a vital part of the team, too. You ALL need to learn to work together.

Lift your organization out of the doldrums with an effective retreat. Any time of the year, retreats are a useful tool for learning, planning, and creative programming.

Chapter Thirteen
Developing A Mission
Statement

Every organization on campus needs a Mission Statement. As a matter of fact, every department and office on campus should have a Mission Statement. While it sounds like a pretty simple matter to create a mission, it's more difficult and requires more thought than you might initially consider.

The modern mission statement is far different than it's predecessor. How can that be? Isn't a mission statement just the purpose for an organization? Shouldn't it be simple to capture your purpose in a few words?

Here's the difference in the modern Mission Statement: it explains why.

Old school mission statements defined what an organization did. Contemporary mission statements define why an organization does what it does.

See, it's really the why we do things that matters.

Let me give you an example. I worked with a history and natural science museum to create a new mission statement. Their old mission was typical. It explained what the museum did: maintained a collection of native plants, animals, and historic buildings and presented programs to the public.

I began the rewrite by asking everyone why the museum was important. I talked with staff, volunteers, board members, visitors, any one who had an opinion. Why was all the stuff the museum did important?

I discovered that the museum had a higher mission than just collecting artifacts. All of the collections were simple tools serving a larger goal.

In the end, this became the new Mission Statement: "The Museum promotes knowledge and understanding of the area's cultural history and natural environment, inspiring people to enrich their lives and build a better community."

The real mission of the organization was to inspire people to enrich their lives, and to thereby create a better community. That was why volunteers gave their time. That was why staff members worked long hours without complaint. That was why donors provided funding. Collecting artifacts and presenting exhibits just assisted in reaching that end goal.

Think about applying that lesson to your organization and office. Take a look at your mission statement. Does it define what you do? Redevelop it so that it explains why you do what you do. What is your ultimate purpose?

Chapter Fourteen
Concepts of Recruitment

In order for an organization to grow, it's important to recruit new members. It can be the hardest part of developing an organization. Below are some steps that current members can follow to help attract new, contributing members to your organization.

Step 1: Clearly Define Your Organization

Have you ever gone to a store to buy a product and the sales person was uninformative and knew very little about the product? When a sales person doesn't know the product, it's impossible to make a sale. The same thing is true when recruiting new members. If you don't have a solid understanding of your organization's goals, activities, and purpose, how are you going to sell your organization and attract new people to join?

Before setting out to recruit new members, make sure you know the following information about your organization:

• What is the group's purpose? (Develop a mission statement.)

• What are the group's future plans? (Set some short and long-term goals.)

• How many people does the group realistically want in order to constructively function as an organization? (Set a target number of how many people you want to recruit.)

By knowing this important information about your organization, you will create a common purpose among current members, which will help them to better explain your organization to others. You may even want to create a flyer or brochure about your organization that contains your mission statement and your goals, as well as past and future activities.

Develop a Mission Statement

A mission statement should state what your organization is and what it does. It should be the basis for all future activities. Here are some tips on how to create an effective mission statement:

• Explain your organization's intentions and priorities.

• Keep it short, concise, and use easy-to-understand language.

• Focus on your final outcome, not the process.

• Use the "Five Whys" method (see chapter nineteen).

• Use your mission statement on all published materials such as flyers, posters, and web sites.

• Review the mission statement regularly to make sure you follow it.

The following is an example of a fictitious mission statement:

"The College Chessmasters' Club seeks to promote Chess by encouraging a greater understanding and a deeper appreciation for the game."

Step 2: Determine a Recruit Profile

After you take time to develop an understanding of your organization, you can then begin to focus on who you want to recruit. You want to make sure that you recruit members who are committed to your organization's purpose and who will be contributing members. Think about the following:

• How will diversity among your members enhance your organization (gender, ethnicity, religion, age...)?

• Is academic major important?

• Is academic level important (For example, an honors society may only want to recruit people with a certain grade point average)?

• Are there any skills or talents you are looking for in members?

• Is there a particular hobby or interest your members should have?

Keep in mind that everyone is entitled to join campus clubs. In deciding on a recruit profile, you are only trying to determine who would be most interested in your club so you can target these people as potential members. However, people you don't expect may be interested in joining.

Step 3: Advertise

Now that you know who you are going to target for new members, you need to start advertising your organization and promoting it to your prospective members.

• Decide what medium would appeal to your new members. For example, if you are creating a music club, you may want to advertise on the campus radio station.

• Is there a certain spot on campus this person is likely to be? For a theater club, the performing arts center would be a logical place to hang flyers. For a math club, perhaps you could get faculty permission to talk about your club during math classes. You might find potential members for the Outdoors Club at the local outfitters' shop.

• What resources, such as time, money, and people does this organization have to give to a publicity campaign? There are also free ways to advertise, such as in the campus newspaper, hanging flyers in appropriate locations, setting up a table in the quad, Club Fair tables, etc.

• What does your organization have to offer prospective members? This is where the flyer you created with your mission statement and activities will come in handy. Distribute this to your future members.

Step 4: Retaining Your Members

Now that you have new members, it's important to keep them interested and active in your organization!

• Have regularly scheduled meetings.

• Be active. Don't forget about the future activities you had planned!

• Keep everyone involved.

• Communicate upcoming events and meetings to all members.

• Be positive! Have fun.

Chapter Fifteen
Presenting a Leadership
Conference

One of the most important programs you can produce for your campus is a Student Leadership Conference. Administrators across the country have recognized the importance of leadership development in college students, and many schools have staff responsible for leadership programs. This is another area where student activities programs are truly co-curricular; it's a prime opportunity for you, the leadership expert, to contribute to the educational mission of the school.

Leadership programs are generally presented in one of three ways: a leadership series, featuring a weekly or monthly seminar on leadership skills; a leadership speaker, coming in to do a single presentation; and, a Leadership Conference, consisting of a number of presentations over the course of one or more days. While each of these programs has benefits, the Leadership Conference offers the most powerful focus on development while highlighting the concept of leadership on your campus.

You should understand, too, that there is no best time for a Leadership Conference. It can work very well at the beginning of the academic year as new officer training. It works equally well at mid-year to reinvigorate your leaders. Even at the end of the year, it functions as advance training for those returning in the Fall. So these programs are always effective and useful for your students.

Target Your Conference

Begin your conference planning by accessing your target audience: the students you seek to develop into leaders. Will it be just the SGA, or will it also include student leaders from other organizations? Will it be open to those students who are not currently involved in campus organizations but who have made a conscious decision to become a leader? How about local high school students: will you also include them in your conference? Including local high school students can be a powerful community outreach for your school and a useful recruiting tool for new students.

Considering your target audience will help you in planning some important initial logistics such as when and where to hold your conference. A conference held during the week can conflict with classes, so you may want to look at other options, such as a weekend program; an evening program; or even presenting the conference over several days to evenly spread the class conflicts. You may also want to consider school holidays such as President's Day or Veteran's Day, or holding your conference the weekend before the semester begins. If the program concept proves popular with the administration, you may even be able to arrange for classes to be canceled for your event in order to increase attendance.

Think about the time frame for your Leadership Conference. Will it be a full day, such as Friday from 9 am until 5 pm? Will it be two half-days, such as Tuesday and Wednesday from 6 pm until 10 pm? Will it be a half-day event, perhaps from 9 am until 1 pm on Saturday? Establishing the length of the conference will determine the number of presentations you'll have, and the time of the conference will determine the need for meal functions.

The location for your Leadership Conference may be obvious on your campus. You may already have a conference center available. If not, then look at your campus facilities while keeping in mind your potential attendance and your program ideas. You'll need at least one room large enough to hold all your delegates. If you do smaller sessions, too, then you'll need two, three or more smaller rooms for break-out sessions. If you'll be serving a meal, then you'll need to consider food services or catering, or availability of restaurants for a quick lunch or dinner.

Program and Topic Decisions

Assess the needs of your target audience and design your program to meet those needs. If you're presenting to your SGA, you may be painfully aware of their leadership shortcomings. If they have trouble with meeting management, decision making, planning and such, then you've got a pretty clear idea of what your Leadership Conference should address.

You may be reaching out to other campus organizations or to the entire student body. In that case, look at expanding your focus beyond simple leadership or procedural training. Not every leader needs to be trained in *Robert's Rules of Order*. Some student leaders may benefit more from personal development programs, such as balancing academics with other responsibilities. An important part of organizational leadership is personal leadership. Helping a leader to be a better person aids that student in being a more effective leader for an organization.

Professional Trainers

You may already have presenters in mind for your conference, perhaps someone you heard or know from other conferences. It's always great to bring in a professional with experience in the college market to serve as your lead speaker. The touring college professionals like me know both what to say and how to say it in order to reach your students-- and that's a skill a corporate trainer may not have.

The professional speaker you bring in should be willing to do multiple presentations, such as the Keynote address plus one or more break-out sessions. This will be the heart of your program, but there is more to be offered.

Reach out to your campus academic leaders, your school president and vice presidents. Deans and other administrators can be a tremendous source for break-out sessions and smaller training programs. Some faculty members are powerful speakers, and trained educators. They can develop and present some excellent programs to supplement your schedule.

Don't forget your own student leaders. If you have experienced and talented student leaders, utilize them. There is nothing like having a peer lead a break-out session. It's a powerful motivator for leaders to present the best session they can. It's also a motivator to younger students to follow the example of your good student leaders.

Remember to keep your sessions a reasonable length. Nobody wants to sit and listen for two hours without a break. As a rule, Keynotes should be about an hour, and break-out sessions should be even less.

Keys to Success

Advance registration is important. Having a registration period well before the conference will let you know how many students will be attending. If more students sign up than you expected then you'll have time to add break-out sessions, increase meal orders, find additional meeting rooms, and more. If fewer people register than you plan, you'll have time to do some recruiting!

Prepare a folder or notebook for each participant, and include the schedule of events, a description of the break-out sessions, biographical material about the presenters, and information about any upcoming events you want them to be aware of, such as ongoing leadership programs or elections. Don't forget to include a notepad and a pen. You'll be surprised at how many students will come empty-handed, with no way to take notes.

Have "roundtable" discussions for each executive position, gathering organization presidents in one room, treasurers in another room, and so on. If you have experienced student leaders, this is a great opportunity for them to facilitate.

Have a "New Leaders" tract, with sessions aimed at those just taking leadership positions. Incoming officers need to know about simple things like agendas and minutes, and they may also need to know about school policies and procedures. New leaders may not know how to reserve meeting rooms; if they can use outside caterers for events; and the other thousand little things that experienced leaders will already know.

Consider some creative break-out sessions. At a student leadership conference in Georgia, I presented a break-out session on low-cost promotion and advertising ideas. Why? Because every organization on campus needs to know how to promote their own events. At another leadership conference in Mississippi I did a break-out session on programming events at a commuter campus. Why? Because campus organizations had difficulty getting attendance at their programs, and that session helped them to understand the dynamics of programming for a commuter campus. At yet another leadership conference in Ohio, I presented a personal achievement and goal setting program. Why? Because effective leaders need to be able to lead themselves before they can lead an organization.

A campus Student Leadership Conference is an excellent way to train your leaders, to reinvigorate your organizations, and to recruit future leaders. It is also a powerful tool in campus collaboration, and is a perfect opportunity for your student activities office to contribute to the educational mission of your school. Plan well, and use your organizational, production, and promotional skills. You'll have students, and faculty, begging for more leadership development opportunities.

Chapter Sixteen
Setting Organizational
Goals

Goal setting is the key to successful organizations. If you don't set goals, then you simply bumble along from day-to-day but never really accomplish anything of substance. Let's take a look at goals, and understand how to use them effectively.

Goals, as you likely know, are the outcome we seek in any endeavor. They are the reason we do what we do. There are basically three types of goals: small, medium and large. Actually, there is one more type of goal, but we'll get to that later.

Small goals are those things we do everyday. Sometimes it's just a "to-do" list, like the simple chores and functions that need to be done in order for an organization to exist.   Scheduling a meeting, preparing the minutes and a meeting agenda, and booking the meeting room are all those small goals.   Simple stuff, really.

Medium goals are bigger, and more important. These are the goals that contribute to the achievement of large goals. Here's an example: reserving the ballroom for your banquet. Just reserving it doesn't make the banquet happen, but it's part of a number of medium sized tasks that must be completed in order to make the large goal happen.

Large goals are the biggest, most important tasks that you under take. They might be planning the Awards Banquet, or they might be a larger service event like pulling together the winning team for the "Relay For Life" cancer walk. Again, these large goals are often the main reason your organization exists.

There are five   steps in setting goals for your organization.

Decide. First of all, you need to decide what you want to do. This is the fun part. I'd suggest you schedule a meeting just for this purpose, early in the year. Brainstorm and discuss various ideas, and remain open to any possibility. At this point, there are no bad ideas or outrageous goals.   It's all about getting input from everyone and just listing them. Don't be afraid to think big!

Clarify. Once you have your list of ideas, determine whether they make sense for your organization. Look at the list of ideas.   Are the ideas important enough to achieve? Do they fit with your mission statement? Do they conflict with other goals?

Prioritize. After you have assembled your list of possible goals, then you have to narrow it down. You can't do them all. Here's the simplest way: it's called "dotmocracy."

Here's an example of how "dotmocracy" works: Imagine that you're seeking five large goals for the year. You begin by posting your list of fifteen goals suggested by your members. You give each member of your organization five sticky dots, the kind you can buy at an office supply store. Every member gets to vote by sticking their dots by the goal they support. If they like a goal a lot, they can stick multiple dots by it. They can put one dot by their five favorite goals. They have five votes, and they can use them in any way they want. Total the votes, and you will have your prioritized list of goals!

Commit. Write down those goals you've brainstormed, clarified, and prioritized,. Put them in big letters on a banner, or on a poster. These are your goals for the year. Make sure you review them at every opportunity. Dedicate your organization's time and energy to achieving those goals.

Act. Finally, take action! Those goals aren't going to achieve themselves. You've got to make it happen. Break the large goals down into medium goals, and break those medium goals down into small goals. Work to achieve the small and medium goals, and the larger goals with become more and more attainable.

Remember that fourth type of goal that I mentioned before? It's known as a "BHAG": a big, hairy audacious goal. BHAGS are *really* big goals. They are possible, but not probable. They are goals you might achieve if you all worked really hard, and worked really smart. They won't be easy to do, but you might be able do it.

Why would you want to set a BHAG? Because they have the power of inspiration. BHAGs are those really outrageous goals, the goals that seem just out of reach, but you know you could do them if you really tried. It's those BHAGs that lift your organization to the next level, help you win national awards, and lead to recognition for your leadership. Don't be afraid to set a BHAG for your organization!

You're likely familiar with the concept of SMART goals. It's a very popular method of goal setting, and you should consider it for your typical goals. It uses the letters of SMART as an acronym for an effective, attainable goal.

S stands for specific. Your goals should be concrete and not abstract. In fact, the more specific you can make your goals, the more likely you are to achieve them. If your goal is to raise money for a charity, state exactly how much you intend to raise. If your goal is a project, specify exactly what that project will be, including the date, time, place, activity, and more.

M stands for measurable. Make sure you set a standard for achievement. You will know you've reached your goal when you've achieved the measurable standard that you set for your goal.

A stands for attainable. Can your goal be accomplished? Is it something that your organization could actually pursue and obtain? That's important, because you will be extending your time and energy striving to achieve this goal. Make sure it's not impossible.

R stands for realistic. Make sure your goal can be accomplished with the resources you have. Think of the time, expense, and labor involved. Is it realistic to believe that you can achieve your goal in the time frame you've set? Do you have the funding to make it happen? Be realistic in your expectations.

T stands for time-based. Set a deadline for your goal. When can you accomplish it? Back that up with a timeline. That is a schedule of what action should be taken and when it should occur. I suggest a "timeline of deadlines." That's my technique of working backwards from the completed project, and setting deadlines along the way to mark important milestones. It's very effective, and will keep you on task.

SMART goal setting is the most popular method of establishing those outcomes you seek to achieve. You'll find it to be a useful means of creating goals that your organization can support and strive to produce.

Goal setting isn't as difficult as you might think, and setting goals is the first step in achieving goals. Here are some final tips in goal setting.

1. Choose goals that are in alignment with your organization's values.

2. Choose goals that are within your organization's capabilities.

3. Don't be afraid of BHAGs.

4. Break a big goal down into a series of medium goals.

5. Never forget: you can achieve any goal you truly believe in.

6. Planning is not enough-- you must take action.

7. Achieving small goals is vital for developing your confidence.

8. Believe in your goals-- otherwise you'll never achieve them.

Chapter Seventeen
Conflict Resolution

Let's look briefly at conflict resolution. Nearly every group has conflicts and disagreements between members. Why are there conflicts? Let me give you five quick causes of conflict:

Interdependence. Every member of an organization depends on other members for help and support.

Differences of Values, Goals, or Beliefs. Members can be diverse, and have widely varying assumptions of worth, what is important, and even basic ideas.

Stress. Members have an important job to do in running their organization on campus. But sometimes they actually have to take exams and write papers, too!

Scarce Resources.   Imagine a meeting when the budget just got slashed *after* the planning was completed. Who gets their project cut?

Uncertainty.   Not knowing the outcome of an issue, problem, or concern.

It can be difficult to resolve conflicts.   One reason is the concept of winning and losing.   If you feel strongly about an issue, then stepping back from that conviction might make you feel as if you lost the conflict.   Nobody likes to lose.

Another reason is sometimes referred to as "zero-sum." That's like a balanced budget, where in order to have one thing you have to eliminate something else.   So, in order for the conflict to be resolved, someone has to give up something.

The last reason conflicts can be difficult to resolve is the famous divorce term: "irreconcilable differences."   At times, the sides just can't be resolved.   In that case, you have to agree to disagree and move on.   When that happens, you can count on conflict recurring.

Conflict Management and Strategies

Here are some ways to handle conflict.   See which strategy works best for you and your organization.

Competition.   Essentially, having each side compete against each other.   You might see this as a discussion and vote on the matter.

Accommodation.   This means finding a way to have both sides win.   It can be tough to do, but it is possible.

Compromise. Basically, people on each side get a part of what they want, while giving up something they want, like a negotiation.

Collaboration. Having both sides work together and come up with a mutually agreeable outcome can be the ultimate team building experience.

Avoidance. Just ignore the conflict. This is usually a bad choice, although it can be an effective solution for certain conflicts.

Negotiation to Resolution

If you are faced with a dispute among your members, you may need to take action. Here are some important things to keep in mind when you are resolving conflicts.

First, prepare for the negotiation. Just because you will be the mediator doesn't mean you can enter the negotiation without adequate preparation. Learn as much as you can about the issue. Learn what is involved, and who is involved. It's important to be ready when you face the two sides.

Second, focus on the process. You do this by keeping the people separate from the problem. If it's a budget matter, that means looking at the budget process and the outcome of that process, not "Brandi wants this much money, and Chad wants this much." Try to take the people-- and the personalities-- out of the problem.

Third, consider the actual issue or interest, not the position. That means look at the Big Picture. For example, what each of the opposing sides wants to do is less important than whether the entire program or project matters.

Ultimately, you want to seek a balanced solution. You may have to pick one side as the winner on occasion. You may find a way to have both sides win sometimes. But true long-term conflict resolution involves compromise and collaboration. The sense that you are fair to both parties in resolving the conflict will go far in reducing future problems between your members.

Plus-- it's the right thing to do.

Chapter Eighteen
The Power of Ceremony

Do you utilize ceremony within your organization? Ritual and ceremony are powerful bonding tools. They result in a sense of community, a feeling of unity far beyond what you might expect.

Think about great organizations, and how effectively they use ceremony, pomp and circumstance. If you've ever pledged a fraternity or sorority, you know all about ritual. But it's really used every day and every where for positive effect, whether we're inaugurating a new President or singing the National Anthem at a ball game.

Understand the reasons you have rituals: to celebrate new members, to recognize a change in leadership, to observe the passing of members, and to acknowledge achievement of goals. These are all important events in the lives of your members. Ceremonies can make them feel even more important.

Start by creating a ceremony to induct new members to your board. It can be as elaborate or as simple as you want, but do something more than just introducing new members at their first meeting.

Don't confuse ritual and ceremony with hazing. You know that hazing is illegal, and more importantly, it's a dangerous and pointless exercise in humiliation. Keep your rituals positive and uplifting.

You might have a minimum requirement of duties prior to official membership, for example, like attending five meetings and working at one event. At that point, the rookies would get their official pin and be welcomed into the membership. Have a pledge or swearing-in ceremony. Have a secret handshake or sign. Do something to make your organizational membership seem as special as it is.

Sound silly? Think about criminal gangs. Don't they have colors, gang signs, handshakes, and more. They don't do that for fun. They do it because it builds a bond between members. That's what you want to do with your ceremonies-- build bonds.

Consider your initiation ritual. It should have recitation of your mission statement or motto, and it should involve the learning of important facts about your organization. If your campus has a convocation ceremony, then you know that's probably where you learned the school fight song, alma mater, and the basic history of your school. That's what you want to happen when you induct new members into your organization.

How about a ritual for changes in leadership? It should be more than just having a new chairperson run the meeting. Create a "pass the gavel" ceremony, when power actually changes hands. Recognize new leaders with a special event or dinner. Greet them with a chant (huzzah!!) or cheer when they take over.

The ever-popular "pass the torch" ceremony can be a powerful symbol of the change in leadership. At the reorganization meeting, begin by darkening the room. Have the current president enter the room with a lit candle. The new president then enters with a new candle. The new candle is lit, and the old candle is extinguished. It's a great analogy for the change in leadership.

When I was president of the Tallahassee Museum, I began every board meeting with a group recitation of the organization's Mission Statement. It was vital for the board to be familiar with the mission of the Museum, and that ritual guaranteed that they said it at least once a month. Plus, I had it printed at the very top of the meeting agenda to symbolize that it was the first thing to consider at every meeting. Literally and figuratively, the mission came before everything else. It was a very effective ritual.

Another powerful ritual deals with "colors." Wearing uniform shirts, the official shirt for your group, separates your members from others. You should seek to have official shirts to wear at events. It doesn't matter if they are basic t-shirts, fancy Polo shirts, or hoodies. The point is to identify your members, and to help them to feel like part of a group.

You might want to consider a ceremony to honor your members who are graduating and leaving the campus. Isn't there a way to recognize your graduating members, to show your appreciation for all of their work on behalf of the organization? Perhaps you can create a new title, a "members emeritus" role for your graduating or transferring members.

Here's an example: You may have heard of a civic organization called the Jaycees. They have chapters all over the world, and perform great service for their communities. But Jaycee membership is restricted to people between the ages of 18 and 41. When a Jaycee turns 42, he or she "age-out" of the organization (become no longer eligible). Such elders are referred to as "Jaycee Graduates," and often serve as advisers and trainers. Before the organization became co-ed, aged-out members were referred to as "exhausted roosters."

Finally, you should have an end-of-the-year awards banquet. This is your opportunity to honor your members for all of their work. You can award plaques for various honors, and recognize those outstanding members and leaders who pushed your group towards achieving your goals.

Don't forget to honor your adviser! He or she may be the hardest working member of your organization.

Ritual and ceremony add gravity and importance to the role of organizational membership. Use it to build community and to bond your members into a cohesive and powerful group.

Chapter Nineteen
The Five Whys

"The Five Whys" is a method of distilling the true cause and/or effect of an issue. Simply put, it involves asking the question "why?," and then asking "why?" of the answer. The pretense is that if asked five times, that simple question will take you to the heart of the matter.

When I first heard of the Five Whys, I was told it was an ancient Chinese technique. Later I learned it was neither ancient nor Chinese; it had been developed by Sakichi Toyota at his automobile company to aid problem solving. Whatever the source, it's a useful tool.

A quick example: My car won't start.

Why? Because the battery is dead.

Why? Because the alternator isn't working.

Why? Because the belt broke.

Why? Because it was worn out.

Why? Because I didn't follow the auto maintenance schedule.

So the root cause of my car failing to start is my own neglect of the required maintenance.

The concept is to peel back the layers of an issue, and get down to the true problem or concern. It also works in helping to determine a purpose. I like to use it to analyze a situation, condition, proposal, or issue.

It's especially useful in developing a purpose or mission statement. While assisting an SGA to create a mission statement, I began by asking them why the SGA existed. "To be the voice of the students," they replied. Why? "So the administration will know the students' opinion on important school issues." Why? "So the school can better meet the students' needs." Why? "So more students can get an education." Why? "So they can become successful productive citizens."

So the SGA's real purpose is to help students become successful productive citizens. That's a totally different idea and more powerful purpose that just being the "voice of the students."

While it may seem a little hokey, and the number five is pretty arbitrary (could be three, could be six), it does seem to work. Maybe looking at the path we've traveled will make the path ahead seem more clear.

The next time you're faced with a decision, issue, or question try the Five Whys. You may just get down to the heart of the matter.

Chapter Twenty
Motivating Others

President Dwight D. Eisenhower said, "Motivation is the art of getting people to do what you want them to do because they want to do it." Truer words were never spoken.

Understand that all motivation is internal, or intrinsic. You can't motivate people through external or extrinsic means. Threatening people is not an effective means of motivating them. What you must do is to find a way to help people motivate themselves.

To get a solid understanding of motivation requires a quick refresher of your high school or college psychology class. Recall "Maslow's Hierarchy of Needs." Abraham Maslow proposed that everyone has the same basic needs, and they must be satisfied in a hierarchical order. Lower needs must be met before higher needs.

The most basic (lowest) needs are physiological needs: air, food, water, sleep, and the other basic requirements of life. According to Maslow, these needs must be met before anything else.

The second level is safety, such as physical security, job security, health, and more. You don't satisfy these needs until the basic needs are met. Think about it like this: People will risk their lives to obtain food, but once they have food they will seek safety.

The third level is love and belonging. The need for love and affiliation is tertiary to basic needs (like food and water) and secondary needs (like safety). But once the lower needs are met, the third level of needs must be satisfied.

Once the first three levels of need have been met, then people seek to satisfy the fourth level: esteem. This is that drive we have to be respected by others, and for self-respect.

The final level of need is called "self-actualization." This is essentially the need to succeed and be productive-- to learn, to solve problems, to be creative. We don't develop those needs until the other (lower) needs are met.

I don't mean for this to be a psychology lesson, but you should understand the most basic motivations in life. All motivation that you seek to instill in others will fit in one of these categories. Your motivational techniques will only be effective if you know the right level of need for the person you are seeking to motivate.

As you seek to motivate others, here are some important first steps. To begin with, you must set a good example. You've heard that before, I'm sure, and it's important. In order to motivate others, they must see the motivation that you have within you to be productive.

Develop good active listening skills. Learn to pay attention and to focus on others when they are speaking to you. Have you ever been trying to talk with someone, and they continue to text others at the same time? You know they aren't really listening.

You should develop your skills so that you listen actively when someone speaks to you. Look him or her in the eye. Nod at the appropriate times, and reply when he or she asks questions. Repeat what the person is saying back to them, "so what you're saying is..." and restate the message. That way you verify your understanding, and it is evident that you have truly been listening.

Set goals for your organization, and reward your staff when they achieve them. Perhaps most importantly, create an atmosphere where good work is encouraged, recognized, and appreciated.

Finally, ask your members what would reward them. You likely can't pay them or give them bonuses. Spend some time at a meeting or retreat and solicit ideas from your members. They can tell you what would motivate them.

You'll find that people can be motivated with a new title, or with additional responsibilities. You might be surprised to learn what will motivate your members.

Chapter Twenty-One
An Attitude of Gratitude

Are you grateful? That's an odd question, for sure. But think about it.   Are you grateful?   Effective leaders express their gratitude strongly and openly.

For reasons too numerous to count, you should be grateful,. Think about it. You're reading this book, so you are literate and educated. You live in a modern world, with freedom and opportunity beyond the wildest imaginations of the people living a century ago. You've got enough to eat, a place to live, likely a car, a phone, a computer, and so much more. Isn't that enough to make you grateful?

Effective leaders are grateful, not just for the material things they have, but for their abilities and for the opportunity to lead. Pause and think of the good things other people have done for you today.   Haven't people helped you today? For example, did someone let you out in traffic, or hold an elevator for you, or say "Bless you" when you sneezed? Of course they did. People are generally gracious and generous of spirit. If you think about it, you have a lot for which to be grateful.

The challenge you face, both as a leader and as a person, is to show *your* appreciation. It really is a challenge, because it's not typically considered an important trait in a leader. However, I believe it is important.

The first step in showing gratitude is to acknowledge it. Recognize when someone is considerate of you, even if, especially if, it's something small. When someone does something for you, say those two magic words: "thank you."

I actually start and end every day with gratitude. The first thing I do in the morning, and the last thing I do at night, is to express my own gratitude. I give thanks. It doesn't matter whether you are religious, spiritual, or not. It's not about who or what you are thanking. It's about embracing an attitude of gratitude. It's about being grateful for who you are and what you have.

While internal gratitude is important, it's also important to apply it externally. You need to thank people, and show sincere appreciation for all they do for you.

Do you write "thank you" notes? I don't mean typing "THX U" and hit send on your cellphone. I'm talking about pen and paper, handwritten notes. They have remarkable power. I've heard that Bryant Gumbel, the famous journalist and sportscaster, begins his day by writing a thank you note. It's the first thing he does when he sits down at his desk each morning. Couldn't you write at least one thank you every day?

Make your gratitude into a ritual. Perhaps you could start each day by listing five things you are grateful for that morning. Just think how powerful that could be, and how that simple act could help you to begin a day of gratitude.

Try hugging people when it's appropriate. You have to be mindful that not everyone wants to be hugged, but a rather surprising number of people really do want to be hugged. I hug people all the time, sometimes people I've just met. And you know what? Sometimes people actually thank me for hugging them!

Make sure you publicly recognize and acknowledge people. As a leader, you need to set an example of appreciation. When someone does good work for your organization, acknowledge them in the act. Then acknowledge them again at the next meeting. Thank people in front of others for their good work.

Give thank-you gifts. Why do people love Oprah? Because she loves her audience, and she demonstrates that love. If you go on her show, she might give you a free car, or new wardrobe of clothes. Wouldn't you love to do that to show others how much you appreciate them?

Well, you can. I assume that you don't have Oprah's budget, but remember the old expression: "It's the thought that counts." It really is the thought that people remember, but the gift makes the memory even stronger.

Here's what I do. I go shopping at the local Dollar Store for items I can use as "creative" thank you gifts. These are just little things that make my thank you note really stick. For example, I might stuff a gift bag with a bottle of aspirin and a bottle of antacids. My note would read "You took care of my headaches and my heartburn when you agreed to serve as the retreat chair." Or how about this one: wrap up a deck of cards and stack of poker chips with a note that says "I wasn't gambling when I asked you to be in charge of the big dance." Or silly plastic flowers, with a note: "This bouquet is made of petrochemicals and will last forever, just like my gratitude for your work." Or how about giving them a "Matchbox" (miniature) car, with a note stating "Oprah shows her gratitude with a free car. I don't have her budget for gifts, but I appreciate you more than you know. So here's a free car from me!"

Is it silly? Sure. Is it cheesy? Certainly. Do people appreciate it? Far beyond your expectations. The person you give that silly toy car will place it on their desk, and every time they see it they will remember your kindness. You will find that from that point on they will be glad to help you any time you need it.

Have you heard the term "random act of kindness"? That means doing something nice for someone you don't even know. Try it! At every opportunity, practice random acts of kindness. When I walk down the street, sometimes I'll put money in expired parking meters. I over-tip in restaurants. I hold doors for people, and let them walk in ahead of me. I let cars out of side streets in heavy traffic. I help people with their bags on airplanes. The truth of the matter is, I don't do it for them. I do it for me. I know that they are grateful, and I like that feeling.

Seek to live a life of gratitude. Everyday you should celebrate your appreciation for all you have-- your family and friends, your health, your life. It's one more way that you lead others.

Afterword

I'd like to sincerely thank you for reading this book. My reason for writing it was to share with you many of the lessons I've learned about leadership throughout my life so far. I'm learning new leadership lessons everyday, and I trust that you are, too.

There is a good reason why the most popular textbook about leadership is called *The Leadership Challenge*, by James M. Kouzes and Barry Z. Posner. Leadership *is* a challenge. It's not a simple task, regardless of the organization you lead. You may work hard setting goals and striving to achieve them. You may experience great success. However, you and your followers are only human. Despite your best efforts, eventually something will go wrong.

Here is one last lesson. When things do go wrong on your watch, whether it's a simple mistake or major blunder, **step up and take the blame.** It may not be your fault. That doesn't matter. You are in charge. As the famous plaque on President Truman's desk read: "The Buck Stops Here." It stops with you.

However, there is an additional step you must make when you accept the blame. **You must take corrective action.** You must do whatever it takes to be sure that the mistake won't happen again. That is vitally important.

We understand that leaders are human, and that mistakes happen. Our biggest concern as followers, is that a mistake doesn't recur. When you take corrective action, you are assuring your followers that you've learned from the error.

Never forget that leadership is an opportunity. It's the chance to have a lasting impact on the world around you, and to make a positive difference in the lives of others. Seize that opportunity, and make this world a better place. That's *your* leadership challenge.

Del Suggs, M.S.Ed.

www.DelSuggs.com
Del@DelSuggs.com

PO Box 2261
Tallahassee, FL 32316-2261

About the Author

Del Suggs has a remarkably multifaceted career as a speaker, an educator, a songwriter, and as a performer. He was voted **"Best Campus Speaker"** by the school membership of the **Association for the Promotion of Campus Activities,** and Del has presented over 600 keynotes, lectures, and training programs for college students across the USA. He has been inducted into the **National Campus Entertainment Hall of Fame**.

He has also earned a *Master's* degree in Instructional Design and Development from Florida State University, where he studied with Dr. Robert Gagne and Dr. Leslie Briggs-- peers of B.F. Skinner. He has taught at Florida State University in both the College of Education *and* the College of Music.

Del is past president of the **Tallahassee Museum of History and Natural Science**, ranked one of the top museums in Florida. He received the **"Museum Service Award for Outstanding Trustee"** from the **Florida Association of Museums.** He has also served on the Board of Directors of the **National Association for Campus Activities (NACA),** the **Florida Flambeau**

Foundation, Inc., and the **Musicians Association of Tallahassee.**

An award-winning **ASCAP** songwriter, singer, and guitarist, Suggs has produced and released six albums of his own music, and he has produced over a dozen releases for his independent label **The Cascades Recording Company.** He has been named "The Very Best of The Best" in music by *Campus Activities* magazine, and performed over 750 concerts at colleges and universities. He's a voting member of the **National Academy of Recording Arts and Sciences** (*The Grammy Awards*).

His volunteer work in various human service, civil rights, environmental, and educational causes has been recognized by a nomination for the **"Harry Chapin Award for Contributions to Humanity"** on three occasions. That is the highest honor the entertainment industry awards for public service. Past recipients include Jackson Browne, Willie Nelson, Ken Kragen (Live Aid), The AIDS Quilt Project, Habitat for Humanity, and Comic Relief.

A prolific author, he has published over 80 journal articles dealing with leadership, campus activities, and Higher Education topics.

Del Suggs is available to speak at your event. You may contact him at:

Del Suggs
PO Box 2261
Tallahassee, FL 32316-2261

www.DelSuggs.com
Del@DelSuggs.com

This book is available for quantity discount for bulk purchase.

For additional copies, contact:

Del Suggs
PO Box 2261
Tallahassee, FL 32316

Del@DelSuggs.com

www.DelSuggs.com